DERIB + JOB

YAKARI
AND THE STRANGER

9th CINEBOOK
The 9th Art Publisher

Original title: Yakari et l'Étranger

Original edition: © LE LOMBARD (Dargaud-Lombard s.a.) 2000, by DERIB + JOB
www.lelombard.com

English translation: © 2007 Cinebook Ltd

Translator: Erica Jeffrey
Lettering and Text layout: Imadjinn sarl
Printed in Spain by Just Colour Graphic

This edition first published in Great Britain in 2007 by
CINEBOOK Ltd
56 Beech Avenue
Canterbury, Kent
CT4 7TA
www.cinebook.com

A CIP catalogue record for this book
is available from the British Library

ISBN: 978-1-905460-27-4

9th CINEBOOK
The 9th Art Publisher

YAKARI AND THE STRANGER

DERIB+JOB

ONE!...TWO!... ONE!...TWO!...

YOU WANTED IT, YOU'LL GET IT! ONE!...TWO!...

ONE!...TWO!... I'M BEGINNING TO GET IT!

AND TO THINK THAT ALL THIS IS JUST FOR FUN...

PFFF!

ONE!... TWO!...

HEE! HEE! HEE!

HOW HE MAKES THEM WORK!

YES, THAT'S WHAT THOUSAND-MOUTHS IS ALWAYS BEST AT!

HERE'S WHERE YOU'RE GOING TO BUILD A FIRST-RATE PLAYHOUSE!

LATER...

WE NEED SOME WOOD! YOU THREE GO GET IT! AND DON'T IDLE ABOUT IN THE HEATHER!

2

WHAT AN IDEA WE HAD...

IF ONLY WE'D KNOWN...

CHOOO!

4

SPLASH

...CHOOOO!

HEY... WHAT ON EARTH IS THAT?

WHO ARE YOU?

?

ME? SNIFF! I'M A...
A...A... A...

CHOOOO!

SNIFF!

...A... A WHITE PELICAN...

...WITH A COLD... SNIFF!

NEVER SEEN A BIRD LIKE THAT!

ME NEITHER!

BUT, WHERE DO YOU COME FROM?

I DON'T KNOW ANYMORE...I'M COMPLETELY LOST...I HAD A TERRIBLE COLD...

AN OLD PELICAN TOLD ME I COULD GET BETTER BY FLYING VERY HIGH...

CHOOO

5

...THEN, SNIFF! I TOOK ALTITUDE. I GOT CAUGHT UP IN THE CLOUDS...

SNIFF!

...I FLEW...AND FLEW... WITHOUT KNOWING WHERE I WAS GOING...SNIFF!

I CAUGHT EVEN MORE OF A COLD IN THE CLOUDS...AND FINALLY I SAW YOU... AND HERE I AM!...A A CHOOO

YOU NEED TO GET BETTER SOMEWHERE ELSE!

WE DON'T NEED A STRANGER HERE BREAKING EVERYTHING!

?

SNIFF!

BUT, THOUSAND-MOUTHS, WE CAN'T LET HIM LEAVE IN THAT CONDITION!

I DIDN'T ASK HIM TO COME HERE!!

ME NEITHER, BUT HERE HE IS!!

A-CHOO

ENOUGH TALKING, YOU TWO!

SNIFF!

THE NIGHT IS COMING AND YOU'VE GOT YOUR FEET IN THE WATER...COME, PELICAN, I'M GOING TO TAKE CARE OF YOU!

SNIFF!

8

WELL, ARE YOU COMING?

SNIFF!

THUMP

SNIFF!

AND WHAT'S MORE, HE DOESN'T KNOW HOW TO WALK!

CHOOOO!

SNIFF!

THIS WON'T WORK! WE'LL NEVER REACH CAMP!...

I'LL PUT HIM ON YOUR BACK, LITTLE THUNDER!

?

9

WELL, AT LEAST MAKE AN EFFORT!

A-CHOOO

FINALLY, AFTER SEVERAL TRIES...

ARE YOU THERE, YAKARI?

YES...

DO YOU WANT TO COME PLAY WITH US?

NO, BUFFALO SEED. I'VE CAUGHT A COLD... CHEEEW

CHOOOO

TOO BAD. COME ON, RAINBOW!

SNIFF!

UH, SNIFF!

YOU NEED TO TAKE CARE OF YOURSELF, YAKARI!

YOU SHOULD GO TO THE SWEAT LODGE!...

GOOD IDEA!

YOU'RE RIGHT, RAINBOW! SEE YOU SOON... AA...

AAAA...

CHOOOO

TOO BAD! WE'LL HAVE TO FIGURE IT OUT OURSELVES!

YAKARI, THIS BIRD IS GOING TO MAKE ME DEAF!

AH!...YOU'RE NOT GOING ON ABOUT THAT, TOO!

SO, WE NEED SOME BRANCHES, SOME ROCKS, AND A GOOD FIRE!

BUT HOW TO BEGIN?

13

WITH THIS!

!

SNIFFLE!

15

17

YES, I THINK I'M BETTER, BUT I'M STARVING TO DEATH!

THAT'S NATURAL, CONSIDERING YOUR CONDITION...

THERE HAVE TO BE SOME FISH...

....IN THIS RIVER...

,,HMM!

16

AH!

!

ZWIP

SPLASH!

A...A...A

18

CHOOEE

OH, NO!!

ALAS, YES! SNIFFLE!

WHAT'S GOING TO BECOME OF HIM?

HE WON'T MAKE IT THROUGH ANOTHER STAY IN THE SWEAT LODGE!

17

IT'S WORSE THAN BEFORE!

GET OUT OF THE WATER FIRST!

A'D I BUST EAT!

HEY! I KNOW SOMEONE WHO KNOWS HOW TO FISH!

GULP! DELICIOUS!

IS THAT ALL?

SNIFFLE!

?!! ?!! ?!?! ?!!

?

THAT'S ENOUGH TO LAST US ALMOST A WHOLE DAY!...

HUH?

BUT I'BE HUGGRY... VERY HUGGRY!

HUH?

SNIFFLE!

OKAY, LET'S GO!

YOU'RE LUCKY THEY'RE SO OBLIGING!

YES, THEY'RE VERY DICE!

SNIFFLE!

BUT...YOU CAD SEE FOR YOUR-SELVES THAT I STILL DEED TO EAT BORE...

MAYBE SO. BUT DON'T COUNT ON US ANYMORE! YOU'RE GOING TO HAVE TO GO FATTEN UP SOMEWHERE ELSE!

SNIFFLE!

UH...LET'S GO; WE'LL LEAVE THESE OTTERS TO REST!...

WE'LL COME BACK LATER—I'M SURE HE'LL BE BETTER!

THAT WOULD AMAZE ME!

CHEEW

WE ALSO NEED TO GET SOME REST, YAKARI!

YOU'RE RIGHT...PELICAN, WE'RE GOING TO LEAVE YOU TO SLEEP QUIETLY IN THE FOREST...YOU WON'T DISTURB ANYONE HERE!

SNIFFLE!

GOODNIGHT, PELICAN!

SLEEP WELL!

BUT THAT NIGHT...

24

A-CHEEEW   CHOOO   CHOOOEE

26

IN THE MORNING...

HIS COLD DIDN'T GO AWAY OVERNIGHT...

CHOOOO

...UNFORTUNATELY. LET'S HOPE THE OTTERS WERE ABLE TO RECOVER AT LEAST!...

25

YAKARI! WE HAVE TO TALK TO YOU! FOLLOW ME!

27

HAVE YOU THOUGHT ABOUT THIS, YAKARI?...

YOU'LL NEVER BE ABLE TO CATCH ENOUGH FISH FOR HIM!

BY MYSELF, NO, BUT WITH THEM, YES!

?

SNIFFLE!

WHO'S "THEM"?

THE BEARS! LET'S GO BACK UP THE RIVER...

A-CHOOEE

*SEE YAKARI AND THE GRIZZLY

31

33

SAY, THERE, YOUR BUDDY REALLY SNORES!

THAT'S A WHISPER... YOU DON'T KNOW WHAT YOU'VE BEEN MISSING!

THE NEXT MORNING...

AAAAAAH! I'M REALLY BETTER!

?!.!?

IT'S TRUE! YOU DIDN'T SNEEZE DURING THE NIGHT...

AND YOU DON'T SOUND FUNNY NOW!

SNIFF...

SNIFF!...

I'M CERTAIN...ABSOLUTELY CERTAIN THAT I'M HEALED!

MAY I?...

...I HAVEN'T FLOWN IN AWHILE...

...I WONDER IF I STILL KNOW HOW!...

IT WORKS! I'LL MEET YOU BACK DOWN ON THE PLAIN...

THANK YOU FOR YOUR HELP, BEAR!

THIS BIRD'S BEEN BROUGHT UP WELL...

HE'S MORE BEAUTIFUL IN THE AIR THAN ON LAND...

UP THERE, HE'S LESS OF A BOTHER TO US!

I'M ALIVE AGAIN!

GLIDING... WHAT EUPHORIA!

BUT NOW IT'S TIME TO TAKE CARE OF BUSINESS WITH THEM DOWN THERE!

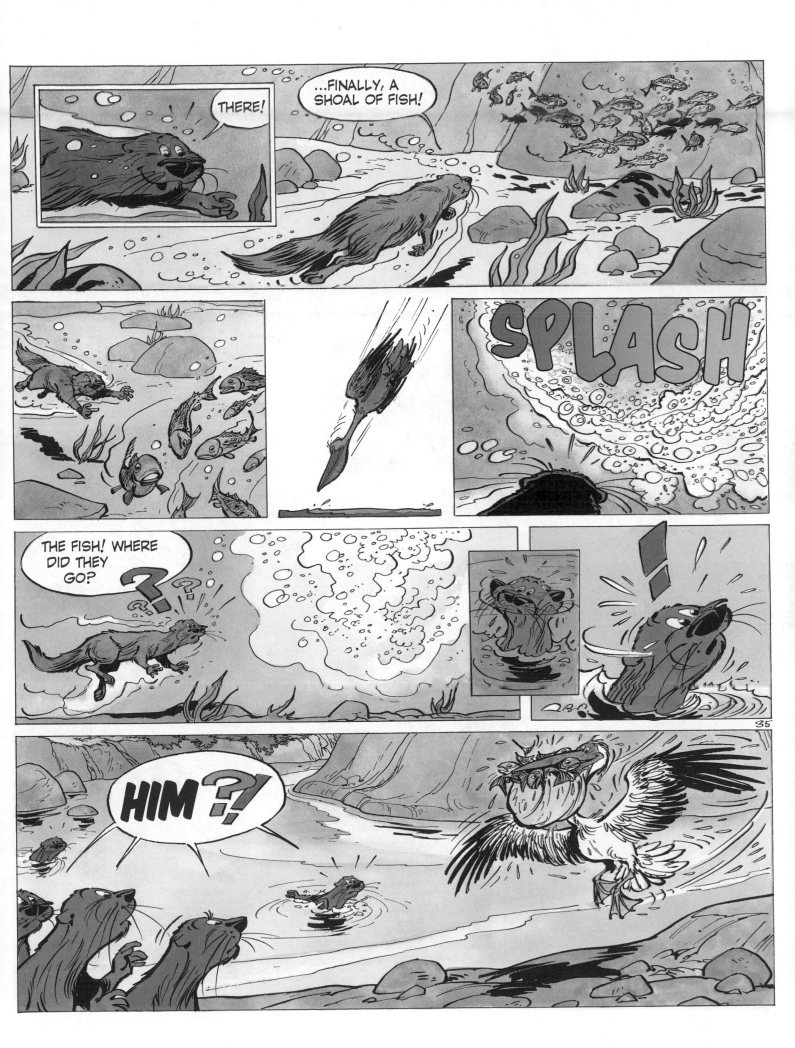

HELLO, MY LITTLE FRIENDS!

OH! PELICAN!

YOU LOOK LIKE YOU'RE IN FINE FORM...

WHAT A PLEASURE TO SEE YOU AGAIN!

WE WERE VERY CONCERNED ABOUT YOU, YOU KNOW...

YOU WERE VERY NICE TO ME. NOW, WE'RE GOING TO HAVE SOME FUN!...

YOU FIRST, LINDEN TREE. CLIMB INTO MY BILL!

?

?!

HOLD ON TIGHT!

37

YIPPEE!

39

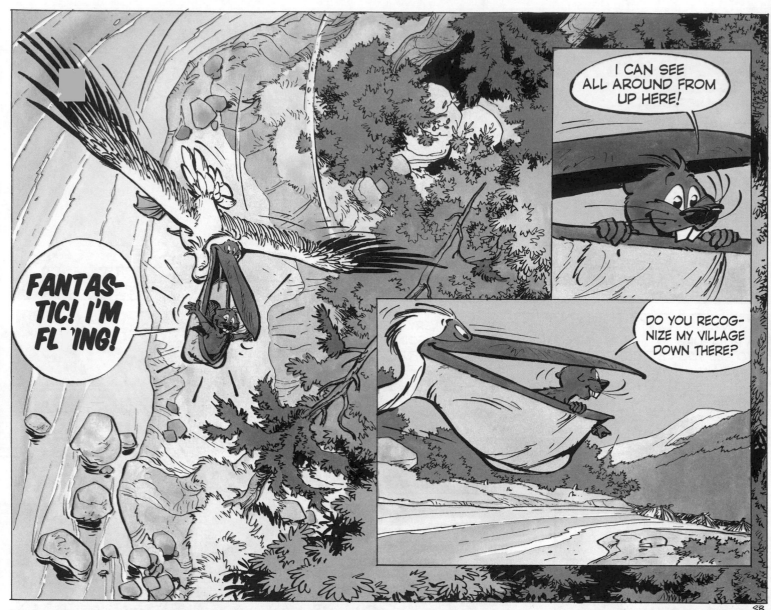

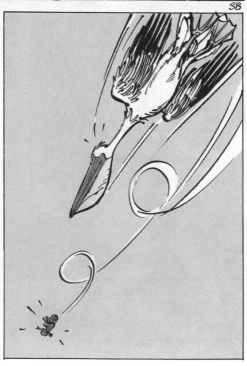

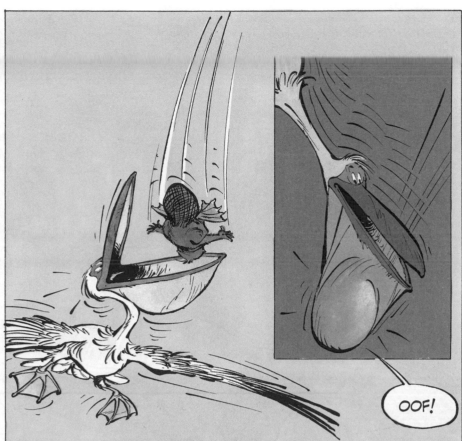

OOF!

THAT MAKES ME LAUGH! CAN WE DO IT AGAIN??

CALM DOWN... CALM DOWN...

LOOK! YAKARI AND LITTLE THUNDER!

WHEE!

!!

UH... H...HELLO!

AND THERE YOU GO!

HE'S GOT THEM EATING OUT OF HIS HAND!

HURRAY FOR THE STRANGER!

YOU SAID IT!

YOU'VE SPOILED OUR LITTLE ONES...

IT WAS A PLEASURE, WOODEN DAM...

...BUT IT'S GETTING TO BE TIME FOR ME TO LEAVE.

THERE'S NO HURRY—TOMORROW'S ANOTHER DAY. STAY AND REST A LITTLE LONGER...

AND THAT NIGHT, EVERYONE IN THE FOREST SLEPT LIKE A LOG...ALL, EXCEPT ONE...

ZZZZZZ

KLAKLAKLAKLAKLAKLAK

42

EARLY THE NEXT MORNING...

?!?

?

?

PELICAN! PELICAN! COME SEE!!

THE END

DERIB + JOB   19 IV 1981